D1364797

TRUSSVILLE PUBLIC LIBRARY
201 PARKWAY DRIVE
TRUSSVILLE, ALA. 35173
(205) 655-2022

TRUSSVILLE PUBLIC LIBRARY
201 PARKWAY DRIVE
TRUSSVILLE, ALA. 35173
(205) 655-2022

0

JENNY'S YELLOW RIBBON

© copyright 1998 by ARO Publishing.
All rights reserved, including the right of reproduction in whole or
in part in any form. Designed and produced by ARO Publishing.
Printed in the U.S.A. P.O. Box 193 Provo, Utah 84603

ISBN 0-89868-364-5–Library Bound
ISBN 0-89868-415-3–Soft Bound
ISBN 0-89868-365-3–Trade

A PREDICTABLE WORD BOOK

JENNY'S YELLOW RIBBON

Story by Janie Spaht Gill, Ph.D.
Illustrations by Lori Anderson Wing

✳ ARO PUBLISHING

TRUSSVILLE PUBLIC LIBRARY

4

Jenny had a yellow ribbon, and she left it on her seat.

Clara Picked it up,
and dropped it in the
street.

A sweeper
sweeping by,
blew it
on a mat.

8

9

The wind blowing by,
blew it on a cat.

11

The cat spun around,
and dropped it on
the ground.

It floated though the air,
and dropped without a sound.

14

15

A dog passing by,
put it in his mouth.

He trotted with the ribbon, back to Jenny's house.

18

He dropped it on the chair,
Jenny saw it when she sat,

21

and now so she won't lose it,
Jenny wears it on her hat.

TRUSSVILLE PUBLIC LIBRARY
201 PARKWAY DRIVE
TRUSSVILLE, ALA. 35173
(205) 655-2022

TRUSSVILLE PUBLIC LIBRARY
201 PARKWAY DRIVE
TRUSSVILLE, ALA. 35173
(205) 655-2022